Andrew James Symington

Some Personal Reminiscences of Carlyle

Andrew James Symington

Some Personal Reminiscences of Carlyle

ISBN/EAN: 9783337057602

Printed in Europe, USA, Canada, Australia, Japan

Cover: Foto ©Raphael Reischuk / pixelio.de

More available books at **www.hansebooks.com**

SOME

PERSONAL REMINISCENCES

OF

CARLYLE.

SOME

PERSONAL REMINISCENCES

OF

CARLYLE.

BY

ANDREW JAMES SYMINGTON.

ALEX. GARDNER,

PAISLEY; AND 12 PATERNOSTER ROW, LONDON.

1886.

CONTENTS.

PREFATORY REMARKS.

———

THE following pages were written immediately after Carlyle's death, and before his Life, Reminiscences, or his wife's Letters had been published. They appeared at the time as a series of papers in the pages of the New York *Independent*. We have since read Froude's various volumes, with mingled feelings of agreement and difference, but without finding occasion to question or modify the impressions we had previously recorded. But so many varied opinions and ignorant condemnations of a great man have, of late, been bandied

about, that some explanation seems to
be called for, in regard to misunder-
standings as to his religious views, his
temperament, and his domestic rela-
tions.   But for the wide promulgation
of such serious mistakes, what we are
now about to say of the latter of these
matters would never have been mooted
by us.

From personal intercourse, extending
over many years, we, in common with all
who came into close contact with him,
know that Carlyle himself was truthful to the core; and, also, that he de-
voutly and reverently accepted the
essential truths of the Christian religion.
True, that, in early student-days, unduly
influenced, as he himself admitted, by
his boundless admiration for Goethe, he
had wavered somewhat in regard to
certain outward matters of form ; but,

though still admiring the great German
poet, he soon lived through that phase,
and, looking back, wrote those verses
comparing himself to a moth that had
singed its wings by fluttering too near
the candle-flame. The root belief in saving truth, to which he firmly clung down
to the end of his days, was substantially that which his godly mother had
taught him. Her strong faith was also
his, though rarely, and then somewhat
enigmatically, formulated by him. As
he himself repeatedly and emphatically
told us, he held fast by the grand old
Bible truths, revealed from heaven, as
the only eternal and veritable realities
on which a man could safely lean with
all his weight. In regard to Carlyle's
religious belief, Mr. Froude did not, and,
unfortunately, from different upbring-
ing, could not understand him.

Health, or rather the want of it, had very much to do with Carlyle's variable moods. He had suffered greatly from dyspepsia, ever since 1818; and had, almost nightly, and often in vain, to fight for sleep. Thus circumstanced, his finely-strung nerves could not but be often on edge; and this, at such times, might give him an air of *brusquerie*, under which appearance, however, his heart was ever tender and true. When out of sorts, through continuous want of sleep, or, when deeply absorbed in his great works, if needlessly intruded on, or interrupted, he, not without reason, would show that he was disturbed, and was then apt to be misunderstood.

Thus, he may, at times, have given even his wife a colourable pretext for fancying herself neglected; but she, knowing better, ought to have made considerate allowances, instead of taking the pet; for it is very certain that he never knowingly, much less intentionally, neglected her. First to last, beyond all doubt, he loved her—devotedly, loyally, and utterly.

Quite as much, however, we are sorry to say, cannot be affirmed of Mrs. Carlyle's strict veracity, loyalty in speaking of her husband, or of her sound common sense. For, although proud of the position which he had attained, with a dash of satisfaction that it more than justified her anticipations, she sometimes felt hurt, and even jealous, at the thought of receiving attention merely as Carlyle's wife, and not for her own personal sake. She, a lady born, and a genius, felt that *she* was also somebody, and was scarcely content to play second fiddle, even to him.

Clever, sharp, shrewd, sarcastic, and a very remarkable woman, of unmistakable genius, she was nevertheless, along with her many good qualities, often very unreasonable and aggravating; taking absurd tantrums and whims into her head, at the causes of which, her husband, try as he would, could at times not even guess, or in the least comprehend; and which, for days together, would make him feel bewildered, wet-blanketed, and very miserable.

Had she only been blessed with a family, it is not unlikely that maternal cares would have absorbed a good deal of her cynicism, diminished unseemly friction, and made her life altogether more sweetly human.

Then, it is well known that she was

wont to indulge in a bad habit of complaining to outsiders of her husband, both in letters and in talk; discussing what she called his inconsiderate treatment of her, dwelling on her exaggerated, or, more frequently, her entirely imaginary ills; conduct unwise and wrong in a wife, even had the allegations been well founded—which hers assuredly were not, although, to her morbid and jaundiced fancy, they at the time might seem to be real.

If her husband, from dyspepsia, sleeplessness, or absorption in study, was sometimes thought by outsiders to be difficult to live with, there was no *if* in her case; she *was* difficult to live with, and, manifestly, with a considerable difference for the worse. Carlyle, first to last, was ever patient and kind to *her*, whatever he might be to idle intruders;

and, instead of resenting or quarrelling
over her manifest and unreasonable
shortcomings, considerately humoured
her every whim, pouring oil on the
troubled waters, and doing what he
could to set matters straight, whenever
he found out what her wishes really
were; for, with heart and hand, he
never ceased loyally to love, honour,
and admire her.　This, not only as to
her freedom of movement, or her re-
quirements, but to such an implicit and
mistaken extent that he trustfully accepted as gospel all her highly-coloured
and often erroneous estimates of people,
when girding at them; endorsing and
unguardedly repeating them as his own.
He thereby, through misplaced faith
in her judgment, unwittingly injured
others, and got himself into bad repute;
for, strange to say, never for one mo-

ment did he suppose that his bright, clever Jeanie's judgment could be at fault. Yet, these estimates were frequently not only unjust, but altogether wrong, biased by her personal pique, and cruelly sarcastic—witness her persistent caricaturing of that worthy Kirkcaldy lady, whom she never forgave for marrying Edward Irving!

After Mrs. Carlyle's death, Carlyle, in the lonely depths of his sorrow, and keen sense of loss, on reading over his wife's Journals, and therein, for the first time, finding recorded how morbidly miserable she had sometimes been, in the same way, accepted it all as gospel, and was overwhelmed with the thought that, now, he could never more explain matters to her, or tell her how very dear she had ever been to him. His soul was filled to overflowing with grief, his tender conscience with remorse; and, sympathetically, he, well-nigh distraught, like Topsy, took guilt to himself for all that was out of joint, where those who had the very best opportunities of judging felt and knew that the fault lay chiefly with her, and that he was little, if at all, to blame.

Hence, people, who had no other means of forming an opinion, on reading those frantic scribblings and self-accusations of his, written, when he was all but demented with grief, in order to obtain relief in mechanical occupation—but which frantic records, when reasonably and rightly read, only speak, through a very thin veil, of his tender conscience—ignorantly and erroneously began to judge him out of his own mouth, and unjustly to regard him even as a monster of cruelty. However, such rash condemnation and inconsiderate abuse is altogether unfair, and entirely opposed to all the facts of the case.

One of the greatest thinkers and teachers of the century, Carlyle's heart was pure, loving, tender, and true; and, even had certain opinions, peculiar, personal traits, or eccentricities of temperament—which, in some form or other, would seem to be inseparable from great originality of mind—actually been the very grave faults which his traducers mistakenly try to make them, these, calmly viewed in the light of his great veracity and sterling virtues, can only be regarded as spots on the sun.

Langside, Glasgow.

PERSONAL REMINISCENCES
OF CARLYLE.

INTRODUCTORY.

On Thursday, the 10th of February, 1881, shortly after noon, all that was mortal of the sage of Chelsea was laid in a corner of the quaint old church-yard at Ecclefechan, beside the honoured dust of his parents and kindred.

Ecclefechan, his native hamlet in Dumfriesshire, lies some ten miles over the Scottish border from Carlisle and sixteen from Dumfries, in a valley surrounded by wooded hills.

The funeral was private and the

cortegé only consisted of the hearse and five mourning coaches. None were present but the immediate relatives; a few friends—such as Froude, Tyndall, and Lecky; and the onlooking villagers. Neither the place nor the day of sepulture had been allowed to transpire, and the general impression of outsiders was that the interment would take place at Haddington, where his wife lies. Snow had fallen in the morning and was followed by rain, so that the day was

" Cold and dark and dreary."

The coffin, of polished oak, bore the following inscription:

THOMAS CARLYLE.
BORN 8TH DECEMBER,
1795.
DIED 5TH FEBRUARY.
1881.

Wreaths of white flowers lay upon it, and the school-house bell tolled slowly as it was being carried to the grave; but ceased when it got there. As the coffin was about to be lowered in solemn silence, the clouds cleared away and a gleam of sunlight burst through the gloom, gleaming on the wet coffin and sparkling on the flowers.

When laid in its place, more flowers were strewn on it, and the grave was filled up by the sexton.

There, in the country quiet of his native Annandale, rather than in West-minster Abbey, interment in which was pressingly offered, Carlyle rests; and, having honestly and nobly done his work, he sleeps well.

Newspapers and magazines, all the world over, with more or less accuracy, will tell the story of his life. Froude, of whom Carlyle once remarked to me that he considered him one of the best-read men in England, probably also Mr. F. Martin, who has devoted years to the subject, and possibly Mrs. Mary Aitken Carlyle, will give us official and authentic records; and innumerable biographies of such a man are sure to make their appearance for centuries to come.

What I now purpose is, neither to write a sketch of his life, nor a criticism of his works, but simply to reproduce from notes a few fragmentary personal reminiscences and impressions, which may not be unacceptable in the way of adding a loose stone or two to the cairn of a great man, who was a moral force to the age, because his heart was as tender and true as his intellect was powerful.

Several members of the Carlyle family have been long and intimately known to me, and at different times been my guests. I also knew Thomas Aird, the poet; with others of Carlyle's old school-fellows and acquaintances, who recollected characteristic traits of his parents. His father died in 1834, and his mother in 1854. Both, I am told, made use of quaint, forcible expressions; so that Carlyle's style was to a large extent inherited. In this respect, his sister, Mrs. Aitken, strikingly resembles him. Having had occasion to be in London, often for weeks together, several times a year, when in business, prior to 1873, I was then always in the habit of visiting at Chelsea, both long before, and since Mrs. Carlyle's death; dating my first visit from somewhere in the fifties.

When Mrs. Carlyle was last in Scotland, I happened to travel in the same train by which she returned to London. About midnight, at a station where there was a stoppage of fifteen minutes, I had gone out to stretch my limbs, and, while pacing up and down the platform, heard myself called by name by some one. On looking about, to ascertain where the voice came from, I saw a lady signalling me from a carriage window; her head was muffled up in a light white woolen shawl, and she proved to be Mrs. Carlyle. On reaching Euston Square Station, I saw her into her own brougham which was waiting her arrival, and accepted a pressing invitation to drink tea with her the following evening, at Chelsea.

Among my treasured relics, I may name—a lock of Carlyle's hair, a MS.

sheet of "Frederick," the quill pen with which he wrote the last chapters of that work (given me by Mrs. Carlyle, on July 15th, 1865), various letters, inscribed books, Carlyle *cartes*, etc.

When Carlyle attended school at Annan, he was boarded with an old shoemaker, named Waugh, quite a character and one of the magistrates of the place. In token of this, the calf-bound copy of Scott's "French Rudiments," from which he learned his lessons and which was given me by his niece, Miss Mary Aiken—now Mrs. Alexander Carlyle—still shows the blotches of shoemakers' resin used to fasten down the paper cover inside the boards. This interesting relic contains his own name and half a page of French, written by himself in 1809, when he was in his fourteenth year. It is curious to compare this early specimen of cali-graphy with his later autographs.

On visiting the house at Chelsea, Carlyle's conversation—whether in the dining-room, drawing-room, or study, sitting at the back of the house, or walk-ing for hours out of doors—was so realistic and strikingly picturesque that, sometimes, on reaching my hotel at night, I was tempted to jot down a few of his more characteristic sayings, while his cogent words and expressions were ringing in my ears.

Long ago, Emerson, speaking of him, (on February 26th, 1848,) remarked to me, that the three things which had most struck him, in his visit to Europe, were: " first, the Townley Gallery Bust of Clytie rising from the Lotus; second, the Conversation of Thomas Carlyle; and, third, to find, in Edinburgh, a man with so much of the spirit of Dante in him as (the late) David Scott, living and working in the nineteenth century."

The house in Great Cheyne Row, where Carlyle dwelt from 1834, when he came south from Craigenputtoch, till his death, was substantially built of good red brick, in the days of Queen Anne. It used to be No. 5, but latterly was numbered 24. Front views of it have often been engraved. Mrs. Allingham has drawn a portrait of Carlyle sitting at the back of his house, and I possess a *carte* of him upon which he himself wrote : " At the back-door, in 1857 (T. C.)".

There was in the Royal Academy Exhibition of 1857 a faithful painting of a room in the house, with striking portraits, entitled " Mr. and Mrs. Carlyle at Home," by Robert Tait, a Scottish artist—a picture which will become invaluable to posterity. If I mistake not, Mrs. Carlyle told me it had been bought by the Ashburtons.

Having jottings of these visits to Chelsea before me, without further preface, I shall now endeavour to convey some idea of how Carlyle looked and talked on some of these interesting and, to me, ever-memorable occasions.

DR. JOHN AITKEN CARLYLE.

On a Saturday afternoon in May, 1863, I went by invitation to spend the evening at Chelsea. Carlyle at once began to speak of his brother, Dr. John Aitken Carlyle, whom I knew and had long corresponded with, chiefly in connection with Icelandic subjects and the old Icelandic translations of the Bible which

I had the pleasure of being able to lend him. Carlyle said, that, after the English Bible, he knew of no translation so good as his brother's prose version of Dante's " Inferno." Five years before, I had received a presentation copy from the Doctor, and, having carefully read it, could appreciate all that he said about it.

Dr. Carlyle was also a good Icelandic and Danish scholar, which led Carlyle to remark that the Danish language was easily acquired by Scotchmen, as, under the skin, it was all Scotch and German.

THE BIBLE.

Reverting to the English Bible, Carlyle said—its translators were honest men, who indulged in no vagaries, but have literal renderings, under pain of eternal damnation. Hence, it is absolutely the best translation in the world. He spoke of the Bible as the grand Old Book, crammed full of all manner of practical wisdom and sublimity—a veritable and articulate divine message for the Heavenward guidance of man.

Referring to the New Version of the Scriptures, then being prepared, he said that, of course, but for such revision, we would not have had our present translation, so that he could not logically oppose it; but, that his whole *feeling* went sorely against the altering of a single word or phrase, for he liked to use the very words his mother had taught him; and that dear old associations should be undisturbed. For long, no book had by him been read so much and so often. It was not only interesting, as matter of fact, and un-approachable in style, but entirely satisfactory; because, while glowing with the divine, it was also intensely human, and, in short, the real thing to which a man could turn for all kinds of need.

He often read through a whole prophet or epistle at a time, so as to take in the scope; and again, at other times, he liked to dwell lovingly and thoughtfully on a single utterance, till its light entered the soul, like a morning sunbeam streaming in through the chink of a closed window-shutter.

HIS HORSE "FRITZ."

He said, he had already been ten years working at "Frederick," and had still eight months' work on it.

He needed exercise, to keep himself
in good working trim, and found riding
suit him. He rode about ten miles
every day. He began to print
" Frederick " when he got his first
horse in town, which he called
" Fritz." First to last, it had carried
him as far as round the Equator.
One day, however, it came down on
its knees. It was trotting along carelessly and not minding its work. He
could not cut it off with a shilling,
after serving him long and faithfully.
At Tattersall's, he could readily have
got £15 for him, but, in that case,
the poor brute would have been
made a hack; so, as an apothecary
in the same street (a man that wanted
to ride a little and would give him fair
usage), offered £9 for him, he jumped
at it, though jockeyship would have got

£50, for he was a well-favoured beast : and, so, he got " Fritz " off his hands.

HIS HUMOUR.

Mr. Carlyle appeared to be in better health and spirits than for a long time. He laughed very heartily, and generally after some quaint semi-conscious re-mark, of his own, full of grim humour, the drollery of which did not seem particularly to strike him till after he, like others, had heard it uttered ; whereupon, for the first time, its full import would apparently begin to dawn upon him.

HISTORICAL ACCURACY.

The idea that Carlyle, in writing history, splashed carelessly, with a big brush, is absurdly untrue. No man was ever more careful in regard to facts; and he earnestly strove to present the very truth, as far as he had attained to see it. He would not say " about such a date," and pass on, .till he had exhausted research in every European library at all likely to aid him. He liked to be able to give day of the month, week, and hour; and, if possible, to add whether there was sunshine or shower at the time.

ABSOLUTE VERACITY.

This characteristic of absolute veracity, he carried out in his letters, and even in the telling of a story. He would return to it again and again, and, like a painter retiring from his easel, gaze, and then, retouching the canvas, bring out many striking effects—never in the way of mere embellishment, but to present the very truth which he wished to convey; and, when he had done, you saw it all before you, and he himself had the satisfaction of feeling it was accurately presented. I have heard him, on such an occasion, say: " There ! That's it ! "

SELF GOVERNMENT.

He invited me to take a walk with him before tea. So we sauntered down by the river, and then along by a square, he the while strongly denouncing so-called self-government, which he said was a Devil's absurdity, and simply meant disorganization, disintegration, and anarchy. It had been carried, said he, a little further on the other side

B

(America); but, there, unlimited land
was, interim, the safety-valve. Here,
however, we saw very plainly whither
it would soon drift us.

ROADS UNDER REPAIR.

The street along which we were passing (King Street, I think) was then under
repair, and Carlyle, waxing wroth, said:
"The roads round here are for ever being
cut up, for something or other—either
drains, gas, or water-pipes. They are
never done pothering, so that one can
never get passing comfortably or peace-
ably along! And why? Because it
seems good in the eyes of a corporate
body of stupid, ignorant, incapable,
clumsy, bad blockheads so to do—men,
the chief business of whose lives seems
to be to meet and dine together four or

more times a year; and the worst of it all is, that they have power—power derived from the powers of darkness and chaos—to levy taxes on the rate-payers to pay for all this madness."

Things, in this way, had come to such a pass that he often looked round, and wondered if he were not in Pandemonium; so much had men perverted the order of God's universe.

THE NORTH.

He then talked of a pleasant visit he had paid to Sir George Sinclair, at Thurso Castle, Caithness-shire; of the Pentland Frith and sea-bathing; of Celts and Northmen; and told me he had often wished to sail north and visit Iceland and other homes and haunts of the Vikings. He had often stood looking north in that direction, and wistfully, too, from the shores of Caithness; but there was no possibility of rest or indulging in longing day-dream possibilities till "Frederick" was off his shoulders; and then, even the desire might be shelved away among the doubtful, drifting category of things to be done "some day."

DRUDGERY.

He next spoke of the arrant folly of people making beasts of burden of themselves, insanely working for Mammon, and dropping down in harness; never enjoying rest or reflection, or pausing for one moment to ask where and whither, or to do aught in the universe but worship self and Mammon, instead of doing a little of the work God has meant everybody to do, in the place and way and time most becoming to a reasonable, immortal being, with a heart in his body, and with human hands, as he has learned to use them.

"When I look round," said he, "it often seems as if the most of people were smitten with madness; and they call it the march of improvement." (Here he burst out into a loud, ironical, hearty laugh.)

WILLIAM BOWIE—ERSKINE OF LINLATHEN.

The conversation then turned to William Bowie, a Paisley weaver, who was in every way a very remarkable man. Quiet, diffident, and retiring, he denied himself much, in order to get books, and was a student of Carlyle's works, finding in them what he could not elsewhere obtain.

I was first introduced to William, when in my teens, by a dear old Paisley friend and companion, the Rev. Wm. Graham, D.D., now Professor of Church History to the English Presbyterian Synod, in London, and I interested myself in him from that period down to the end of his life. Latterly, some years before his death, he left the loom, having obtained better employment from some kind friends at a bleach work. When Carlyle's sister, Mrs. Aitken, was on a visit to me, I got William Bowie to meet her, and, after that, they corresponded together. His letters were full of thought and tersely expressed. I possess several hundreds of them. Bowie, who knew of Carlyle through a mutual friend, the late Thomas Ballantyne, had long ago sent a letter to Chelsea, written from the depths of a grateful heart. This letter interested Carlyle so much that he sent it to his friend Erskine, of Linlathen, requesting him to go and look up William Bowie. To this communication, Erskine sent the following reply, which is now for the first time printed from the original :—

"Cadder, Glasgow, 10th Feb., 1840.

"*Dear Mr. Carlyle :*—Your very welcome letter and its companions, after some calls by the way, found me in Edinburgh, where, having no home and many acquaintances, I never have time for anything but walking from one house to another.

"I am now back in the west country, and I propose speedily to seek out William Bowie. I am much struck by his letter. It is a comfort to find any of these hard-wrought drudges discovering that there is another way of freeing and

righting themselves than by following
John Frost; aye, and discovering, not-
withstanding the dinginess of their own
special holes, that they are in a real
divine temple, full of significance. Our
weaver is in the high way of becoming
a priest in the Temple, offering himself
up a living sacrifice, as the tent-maker
says, for he seems to regard knowledge
in a practical way, desiring direction,
because he knows he is on a journey and
may go wrong, and must, if he has no
direction.

"You do Scottish benevolence great
injustice in taking me as the represen-
tative of it; but I shall go to Paisley
and enquire after our friend. I have
often heard of you since I saw you; but
it is a great pleasure to hear a word
direct. I am very much obliged to you
and Mrs. Carlyle for remembering me.
I remember you both with much love
and regard, and join in William's prayer
for you—that the God of peace may rest
and abide with you and strengthen you
in every good word and work.

"I have read 'Chartism' with much

sympathy. I believe that no legislative acts, no state nostrums can do us any good. I believe that each man must do his duty and fill his place, recognizing himself to be in a temple and called to be a priest in it.

"I have read your Miscellanies, also, and could say something, like William Bowie, about them.

" Give my affectionate regards to Mrs. Carlyle, and believe me

" Yours, very truly,

T. ERSKINE.

"P.S.—This is our poor young Queen's marriage-day—'too young' for these strange times."

The visit was made to Paisley, and William Bowie was found by Erskine, in ability, insight, and worth, to be all and more than he expected. The two were mutually delighted with each other, and a number of friendly letters passed between them, all of which I was privileged to read.

After his visit to William Bowie, Erskine thus wrote :—*

"Cadder, 7th April, 1840.
" Dear Mr. Carlyle,
        " I ought before now to have given you tidings of your friend William Bowie.   The first time that I called on him, he was not at home, but I saw his host and hostess, from whom I extracted what information I could.   They spoke well and kindly of him, calling him a *quiet* lad that was very fond of books. They said that his mother was an excellent, sensible woman ; and his grandfather and grandmother *just first-rate folk, capital folk out of Ayrshire.*

"Fine, cracky, sociable bodies, the host and hostess were, and the interest that they took in their lodger and in his

---

* Copied from the original letter, and, so far as I know, it now appears here for the first time.—A. J. S.

forebears impressed me favourably of him.

" When I next called, I found him in, and I found him, in truth, a very quiet lad, a good deal isolated, liked by the people that are close to him, but understood or sympathized with by few, if any.

" Your ' Miscellanies' were lying on his table, and I found it introduction enough to his confidence, to profess myself a reader of your books. After sitting with him a little while, I told him that I knew you, which gave him great pleasure, and drew from him the acknowledgment that he had written to you and had received an answer.

" He was very inquisitive to know everything about you that I could tell him, and seemed to have formed his own picture of you already from your writings, which he often quoted with great delight, and with a look of kindly humourousness, indicating that he entered into the meaning, such as you never see on any other than a Scotch face,

" I afterwards called on him at his workshop, poor fellow, and got him out to take a walk with me. I like him, and intend to see him from time to time, and have given him my address that he may write to me, if he likes, at any time. Mr. Scott also has seen him and likes him.

"I have heard that you intend to give a course of lectures this spring — is it allowable to ask what the subject is? I should like, if I could, to take a run up to London, and perhaps I may. It is long since I have seen you and Mrs. Carlyle. I hope she is better and stronger than when I last called at Cheyne Row. With best wishes to you both,

  " I remain,
   " Yours most truly,
    " T. ERSKINE."

Carlyle, on this occasion, asked me all about William Bowie's antecedents, etc.; and, having obtained such particulars as I could tell him of his sad,

lonely history, his aspirations and sur-
roundings, he added :

" Poor fellow ! He kept by himself
through life, and thought; when we and
other idiots were babbling and joining
the insane throng—swelling the noise
with words not always better than the
silences. Peace to poor William ! "

GOOD BREAD—ROYAL SOCIETY— DARWINIAN THEORY.

On returning to tea from our walk,
there was a loaf of home-baked brown
bread on the table, which loaf led to a
discussion on fermentation and yeast.
Carlyle remarked that, with all the
boasting of science, that simple thing
was not understood here. We had to
get German yeast three times a week
from Hamburg. Could not make it
here.

There was a Guild of Bakers to supply bread to the people—bad, indigestible bread, often not fit for food. Yet government, although it was their function, did nothing to find out why it was bad and have it made right. This forsooth was self-government and liberty! Anybody could in two hours learn to make better bread at home than bakers could or would do.

The Royal Society, French Academy, British Association & Co. could speak grandly, and tell us learnedly how the world, or the universe itself was made, or not made; and, if there were any prospect of its paying, he doubted not but they would set about the attempt to make one. They had confidence and daring to that extent, and presumption for anything, provided it be only sufficiently distant and didn't immediately concern them. But here, as to a simple matter which comes home to our daily necessities (how to make good bread), it was quite below their notice. He could not get a so-called scientific man to consider it. Perhaps Dr. Robert Angus Smith would. He was more hopeful of him, than of any he had talked with on that or other practical subjects. He then went on to say to me, in words which have already appeared elsewhere, signed " Veritas," but which are the only part of these jottings ever before printed: " The short, simple, but sublime account of Creation given in the first chapter of Genesis is in advance of all theories, for it is God's Truth and, as such, the only key to the mystery. It ought to satisfy the savans, who, in any case, would never find out any other, although they might dream about it. Then, alluding to the development hypothesis, waxing warm, and, at the same time bringing his hand down on the table with a thump like the sledge-hammer of Thor, he emphatically added: 'I have no patience whatever with these GORILLA DAMNIFICATIONS OF HUMANITY!'"

MRS. CARLYLE

Mrs. Carlyle was sharp, clever, brilliant, often extreme and unreasonable in her prejudices, and inclined to be sarcastic. She had also the power of inoculating Carlyle, who implicitly believed in her judgment, with her views. Consequently, she made the balls, and he fired them, without any questioning or misgiving whatever as to their rightness.

EARLY DIFFICULTIES IN FINDING PUBLISHERS.

Carlyle talked quite freely about the difficulties he had to encounter in getting publishers to undertake, or even to look at, his early books. "Respectable medio-crity," said he, "gets comfortably along; but extra goodness, whether it consist in newness or truth, matter or manner, shares the waste-paper basket with bad-ness, because no difference is perceived between them by the wiseacres. *Sartor* went its rounds, for long, al-most hopelessly. America ventured to make a book of it, and also to collect my essays into volumes, before that service was done for them in this country. Less tied down by the conventionalities, said he, they ventured to think for themselves, and give an opinion which

c

has, to some extent, been confirmed on this side."

" Some time ago a London publisher offered to purchase a copyright of him ; but he said : ' No ; thank you, sir ! Once on a day, I would have been glad of any kind of offer, but could get none. Now, when I publish, it is *my* book that is wanted, and it matters not, to those who ask for it, whether the publisher be Tom, Dick, or Harry. So I shall retain the copyright, in order that I, or those in whom I am interested, may reap the reward of a life of no little labour.' "

EFFECTS OF MENTAL STRUGGLES IN STUDENT DAYS.

He then alluded to the mental struggle which he had undergone in his student days, when choosing his path, at what he called "the cross roads of life." It, to him, was "a Gethsemane" and it had left its mark indelibly upon him; indeed, from that time, he had scarcely known what it was to be entirely free from dyspepsia. His nervous system, too, was painfully sensitive to noises, and sometimes sleep would altogether elude him for a succession of nights, and had to be fought for in various ways—often by walking for hours out-of-doors late at night, to weary himself by physical exercise. When such restless fits were on him and long protracted, he said that, in addition to his being absorbed think-ing about his work, he, from natural causes, sometimes was apt to be a little crusty. At such times, we have heard Mrs. Carlyle, make some little remark, bearing on his wants or wishes, so irresistibly droll, that, in spite of his grim visage, she would compel him to roar with laughter, and, the spell thus broken, he was all right again.

LARGE PAINTING OF FREDERICK.

Mrs. Carlyle showed me a large oil painting of Frederick, hanging on the south wall of the drawing-room (the original of that engraved as the frontispiece of her husband's work). It had been presented to her by Lord Ashburton.

ICELAND — THE NORTHMEN — MRS. CARLYLE'S FRIENDS—ICELANDIC DICTIONARY — INTENDED VISIT TO ORKNEY AND SHETLAND.

Carlyle told me, he had read my "Icelandic Book,"* saying some kind,

---

* *Pen and Pencil Sketches of Faröe and Iceland*: Longmans.

friendly things about it, and adding that he had always had a craze about these regions. "The old Northmen," said he, "whatever else they had, did not lack deeds, and notable ones too. Their swords did not smite the air."

Mrs. Carlyle enquired of me, curiously, regarding the people I had met in Faröe and Iceland; and, on my telling her that they were intelligent, truthful, hospitable, and friendly, she clasped her hands, and, with upturned eyes, like a Madonna, exclaimed — "Oh! how I should like to go there, and make some new friends; for I am so utterly, and heartily, tired of all my old ones!"

Carlyle then spoke about material towards an Icelandic Dictionary, which the late Mr. Cleasby collected in Iceland and Copenhagen, and had left in MS.: and I promised to make in-

quiries and ask Professor Rafn, of
Copenhagen, with whom I was in cor-
respondence, about it. (It has since
that time been completed and enlarged
by Gudbrand Vigfusson, and issued
from the Clarendon Press, at Oxford,
1879).

Iceland was too far away for him to
visit now, he said; but he wanted to
take a sea voyage and had thoughts of
visiting Orkney and Shetland, towards
which he had often looked, with
longing eyes, from Sir George Sinclair's
place at Thurso. His brother the
Doctor would accompany him. Would
I be at the trouble to find out the
sailing of the steamers, jot down the
route for him, and name people who
would be able to give him local
information? This I did for him, on my

return home, and sent on the result to
Dr. John A. Carlyle.

MRS. CARLYLE MAKES AN APPOINTMENT.

Mrs. Carlyle had previously written,
asking me, before coming to tea
at Chelsea, to meet her and some
friends at the Crystal Palace; but she
had been prevented from keeping the
appointment by callers. On reaching
the house, after apologizing and
explaining, she added, that, knowing I
had gone there solely on her account
and would be waiting for her, she had
been profoundly miserable about it—*for
the space of ten minutes!*

FREDERICK A LABORIOUS UNDERTAKING.

Referring to " Frederick," Carlyle

said: "This book business is an awful weight on me. I had no idea of the enormous labour it involved, when I began it, or, would have at least paused, before putting my hand to the plough."

CARLYLE METHODICAL.

As I had a call to make, five miles off, diagonally across London, Carlyle fetched a map and assisted me to pilot my route on it. The bundle of maps from which he took it, I observed, was arranged in a most orderly manner for reference, and neatly tied up with red tape.

DRESS AND APPEARANCE—WORK.

He was habited in a gray tweed dressing-gown; his hair, beard, and moustache gray, grizzled, and longish.

On parting with him at twenty minutes past nine o'clock, he came out to the street-door, with his bare head, bidding me good-night, with a very hearty shake of the hand and a pressing invitation to come again before I left town.

That year, he got through an amazing amount of work, and in a letter received from him, in July, he alludes to his being "still in a whirlpool of hurries."

ICELANDIC PTARMIGAN.

Having in December received some ptarmigan from Iceland, I forwarded a brace to Chelsea; and, in a letter acknowledging them, Mr. Carlyle wrote (on December 26th, 1863):

" Your two birds arrived safe—ex-

cellent birds, of new foreign flavour—
and did duty here yesterday, keeping
Xmas far away from home. Thanks
for that mark of your attention. My
wife has had a bad fit of illness, and,
indeed, still has, tho' now, we hope,
recovering.

"With many thanks and good wishes,
"Yours sincerely,
"T. CARLYLE."

PREPARATIONS FOR INAUGURAL ADDRESS.

In 1866 Carlyle had before him the
delivery of the inaugural address at his
installation as Lord Rector of Edinburgh
University.

That year I saw him at Chelsea, both
before and after his memorable visit to
Scotland. He was extremely anxious,
if he carried out his reluctant intention
of appearing before the students, to say

something which would really be serviceable to them.   A sense of duty
urged him, although he shrank from
public appearance, and said he felt as
if he were going to be hanged.   So he
dictated an address to his amanuensis ;
but, on looking at it, was altogether
dissatisfied with the result, remarking
that, if he could not do better than that,
he must abandon the business.   He
tried again ; but, still dissatisfied, set
aside and blotted from his mind everything he had planned in the shape of
MS. preparation, and resolved to say a
few simple words to the young men,
coming directly from his heart, and such
as would naturally occur to him at the
time.   And, so, we have those im-
pressive words spoken on that occasion,
which those who heard will never for-
get.

GREAT DEMAND FOR TICKETS OF ADMISSION.

From far and near, orders of admission to the Installation Hall in Edinburgh were in urgent demand and not to be had. Desiring to take my friend, Dr. David Mackinlay, who had once spent an evening at Chelsea with me, I applied in influential quarters for two tickets. However, only one came, which I resolved to give up to him. Then it occurred to me that perhaps Carlyle himself might be able to secure my admission ; this he kindly did, sending an autograph order by return of post.

PLATFORM IN THE INSTALLATION HALL.

His brother, Dr. J. A. Carlyle, Dr.

David Mackinlay, and I, went to the hall together, and there witnessed the splendid and unique ovation paid to the greatest literary man then alive by his *Alma Mater*.

On the platform, we saw the Principal of the University, Sir David Brewster, who in other days, as editor, had got the young student to contribute articles to the "Edinburgh Encyclopædia." There, too, sat Dr. Guthrie; Sir George Harvey, P.R.S.A.; Tyndall; Huxley; Erskine, of Linlathen; Lord Provost Chambers; Dr. Rae, the Arctic explorer; and many other men of world-wide renown, all assembled to do honour to the new Lord Rector.

OF THE ADDRESS.

When Carlyle, characteristically throwing off his official robe of office, came forward to speak, he was evidently thinking of days long gone by; and the low tone of his voice and whole manner indicated that he was profoundly moved. Soon, however, getting absorbed in thoughts about the young men before him, he fell into a simple colloquial tone, and uttered wise, practical, helpful words, with a paternal depth and tenderness of feeling, in his old, homely Annandale accent, which half a life-time's residence in London had in no way changed, earnestly exhorting them to fight the good fight and quit themselves like men; to love wisdom for its own sake, piously, valiantly, humbly, beyond life itself, or the prizes of life—then all would be well with them; closing the whole with a marvellous recitation of a few lines from Goethe—holding the vast audience silently spell-bound, thrilling it electrically through and through with a powerful eloquence beyond the reach of art, and Nature's very own.

RECEIVES NEWS OF THE SUDDEN DEATH OF HIS WIFE.

Shortly after this memorable occasion, on April 21,—when visiting his sister and brother-in-law (the Aitkens) at The Hill, Dumfries,—like a bomb-shell, came the telegram which announced the sudden death of his wife, in London. He had tossed it unopened to his sister, who, tearing it open, read, turned pale, and silently passed it back to her brother. Having read it, unable to utter a word, Carlyle rose from the table, retired to his room upstairs, shut the door, audibly agonized in prayer for a time; and then,

this brave, heroic, Spartan soul descend-
ed, finished his cup of coffee, and at
once proceeded to arrange and do what
had to be done, retaining the mastery of
himself, although his heart was breaking, and the light of his life had gone
out.

True sympathy was not wanting to
the lonely veteran in his sore affliction,
and condolences reached him from all
quarters, from Her Gracious Majesty
downward.

VISIT TO CHELSEA—REFERENCES TO THE STUDENTS AT EDINBURGH.

On my first visit to Chelsea after his
bereavement, no allusion whatever was
made to it on either side. I knew he
could not trust himself to touch on it.

He talked freely about other things,

described his feelings when addressing the students at Edinburgh, and how he sympathized with them in aspirations that might never be attained, and in possibilities beyond their ken, and dis-appointments and sufferings, which last were very certain. He had travelled the road before them, poor young fellows! Their loyal attitude, that day, touched him ; but he felt that he could do little for them beyond urging them honestly to do their duty by God and man, and to do so with a brave heart, through good report and bad report, working with all their might at what lay nearest them, for genius, which throve, had always a large capacity for work.

LIBRARY AT WINDSOR—PRINCE ALBERT.

He mentioned that, years before, when

D

Her Majesty first heard that he was en-
gaged on " Frederick," she kindly had
intimation sent him that the library at
Windsor was at his service.   One day,
when there, the librarian gave him a
hint that the Queen would like to meet
him, and would probably look in that
day; but this had quite a different effect
on Carlyle from that which the librarian
intended or expected.   The shy student
at once withdrew.

On another occasion Prince Albert,
who, as he afterward found, had specially requested of the librarian to be
notified of his (Carlyle's) presence at
Windsor, surprised him in the library
and had a pleasant chat.   Carlyle said
that the Prince was dressed in a plain
suit of tweed and was a very well-
informed, sensible, gentlemanly man,

unaffected, simple, friendly, and kindly in his manner.

MEETS THE QUEEN AND ONE OF THE PRINCESSES AT THE DEANERY OF WESTMINSTER.

He also told me, of his friends the Dean of Westminster and Lady Augusta Stanley, asking him to lunch; and his there meeting Her Majesty, of whom he always spoke with loyal affection and respect.

He also wrote a remarkable letter giving a most vivid account of this interview with Her Majesty, which account we were privileged to read. As an artistically etched word-portrait, nothing could be finer, more truthful, or valuable, for future history.

His description of his taking one of

the princesses, on his arm, in to lunch, was as amusing as it was graphic.

"She was," said he, "a kind-hearted, nice, bit lassie, with no pride about her; but several times I saw her taking a curious side-glint at me, and no doubt she was wondering in her own mind why on earth she was consigned to the care of such a rough old curmudgeon as I am, instead of to somebody or other more like herself."

HIS AVERSION TO GO INTO GENERAL SOCIETY.

Even during Mrs. Carlyle's life, Carlyle oftener than not refused invitations; and frequently, when they had been accepted, apologies were sent at the eleventh hour. Formal dinners he disliked. A talk over a quiet cup of tea had more chance to lure him; but he cordially hated being lionized in any form. To Mr. Froude, who was once urging him to meet some distinguished individual (I think it was Lady Salisbury), who had a great desire to see him, he said; "If the Virgin Mary were to ask me to dine with her, it could do me no good!" Knowing this, his aversion to go out, and also the chance of his forgetting all about such engagements, on the day when he was expected, his friends would sometimes drop in or send him a reminder, to make sure of him. We possess such a reminder, in the shape of one of Lady Augusta Stanley's calling cards, with a kindly message for him written upon it by her, and which she left at his door.

VISIT WITH DR. ROBERT ANGUS SMITH, F.R.S.

One evening in 1868 I went to Chelsea, accompanied by my old friend, Dr. R. Angus Smith, F.R.S. We found Carlyle's sister, Mrs. Aitken. She went up-stairs to the drawing-room to waken her brother, who was taking his siesta on the sofa.

When we shortly afterward joined him, he told us he had been reading "Meister" and the Queen's book. He seemed a little tired and taciturn at first, yawned and rubbed his eyes; but he soon melted into a most kind, amiable, and easy mood, talking fluently, genially, picturesquely, and dashing his quaint remarks with a drollery peculiarly his own,

OF RAILWAY TRAVELLING.

Speaking of locomotives and rail-
ways, which he personally disliked, he
compared the age to the vision of
Ezekiel's wheels, and gave a ludicrous
description of a short railway journey
he had once taken with his brother,
the Doctor, remarking of the train:
"What is it but a metallic devil?
while the screaming and howling of
steam-whistles were like as if a million
fiends were running to and fro over the
earth!" He then declared, laughing
heartily, the while, at his own grotesque
exaggeration, that, if he had had only
one leg, he would rather hop on it, to
all eternity, than again venture on a
journey by the Metropolitan Railway,
with its nerve-edge-setting multiform
hubbub and jumble of noises, shaking,

ear-piercing screams, and Stygian stenches.

" *WILHELM MEISTER.* "

"Meister" he characterized as the finest book on education ever written.

LETTER FROM MR. DIXON.

He had recently received a letter from Mr. Dixon, an intelligent cork-cutter at Sunderland, which he read to us, requesting us to procure certain information for him, in order to enable him to answer it from correct data.

CARLYLE ON READING.

Carlyle, although resenting needless intrusion, kind and tender-hearted, was always ready to give a word of advice, or money help, where he deemed that either was really required. To do so efficiently, he would put himself to no end of trouble, and this in cases where he could look for no return but the satisfaction of doing what he considered right. The following letter, which he wrote fifteen years before, in answer to a correspondent who had asked his advice, finely illustrates this trait: it had, somehow, got into print, and Carlyle used, on fitting occasions, to send copies of it to correspondents :—

Chelsea, March 13, 1843.

Dear Sir,—Some time ago your letter was delivered to me ; I take literally the first free half-hour I have had since, to write you a word of answer. It would give me true satisfaction could any advice of mine contribute to forward you in your honourable course of self-improvement ; but a long experience has taught me that advice can profit but little; that there is a good reason why "advice is so seldom followed "—this reason, namely, that it is so seldom, and can almost never be, rightly given. No man knows the state of another; it is always to some more or less imaginary man that the wisest and most honest adviser is speaking. As to the books which you, whom I know so little of, should read, there is hardly anything definite that can be said. For one thing, you may be strenuously advised to keep reading. Any good book, any book that is wiser than yourself, will teach you something—a great many things, indirectly and directly—if your mind be open to learn. This old counsel of Johnson's is also good and universally applicable—read the book you do honestly feel a wish and curiosity to read. The very wish and curiosity indicate that you then and there are the person likely to get good of it. "Our wishes are pre-sentments of our capabilities." That is a noble saying, of deep encouragement to all true men; applicable to our wishes and efforts in regard to reading, as to other things. Among all the objects that look wonderful and beautiful to you, follow with fresh hope the one that looks wonderfullest, beautifullest. You will gradually, by various trials (which trials see that you make honest, manful ones, not silly, short, fitful ones), discover what is for you the wonderfullest, beautifullest; what is your true element and promise, and be able to abide by that. True desire, the monition of nature, is much to be attended to. But here also you are to discriminate carefully between true desire and false. The medical men tell us we should eat what we truly have an appetite for; but what we only falsely have an appetite for we should resolutely avoid. It is very true. And flimsy, "desultory" readers, who fly from foolish book to foolish book, and get good of none, but mischief of all— are not these as foolish, unhealthy eaters, who mistake their superficial, false desire after spiceries and confectioneries for the real appetite, of which

even they are not destitute, though it
lies far deeper, far quieter, after solid
nutritive food? With these illustra-
tions I will recommend Johnson's
advice to you.

Another thing, and only one other, I
will say. All books are properly the
record of the history of past men.
What thoughts past men had in them;
what actions past men did—the sum-
mary of all books whatsoever lies there.
It is on this ground that the class of
books specially named history can be
safely recommended as the basis of all
study of books; the preliminary to all
right and full understanding of anything
we can expect to find in books. Past
history—and especially the past history
of one's own native country—everybody may be advised to begin with
that. Let him study that faithfully, innumerable inquiries, with due indica-
tions, will branch out from it ; he has a
broad, beaten highway, from which all
the country is more or less visible—
there travelling, let him choose where
he will dwell. Neither let mistakes nor

wrong directions, of which every man, in his studies and elsewhere, falls into many, discourage you. There is precious instruction to be got by finding that we were wrong. Let a man try faithfully, manfully, to be right; he will grow daily more and more right. It is at bottom the condition on which all men have to cultivate themselves. Our very walking is an incessant falling, and a catching of ourselves before we come actually to the pavement! It is emblematic of all things a man does. In conclusion, I will remind you that it is not by books alone, or by books chiefly, that a man becomes in all points a man. Study to do faithfully whatsoever thing in your actual situation, there and now, you find expressly or tacitly laid to your charge—that is your post; stand in it like a true soldier; silently devour the many chagrins of it, as all human situations have many; and be your aim not to quit it without doing all that it, at least, required of you. A man perfects himself by work much more than by reading. They are a growing kind of men that can wisely combine the two things; wisely, valiantly, can do what is laid in their hand in their present sphere, and prepare themselves withal for doing other wider things, if such lie before them. With many good wishes and encouragement, I remain, yours sincerely,

THOMAS CARLYLE.

Chelsea, March 13, 1843.

LETTER FROM CARLYLE TO HENRY F. CHORLEY.

The following letter was written in July 1867, upon receipt of an intimation from Henry F. Chorley that, under the will of his recently deceased brother John Chorley (the eminent Spanish scholar), Mr. Carlyle was entitled to a bequest of a thousand pounds. The letter speaks for itself, evidencing pure unselfishness and true nobility of soul, on the part of the writer :—

Chelsea, 11th July, 1867.

Dear Sir,—It is infinitely affecting to me, this generous message from him who is now gone far away! How little I deserved it of him, how un-expected it is, how little needed now, though so good and noble!

My Banker's name is " S. Adamson, Esq., British Linen Company Bank, Dumfries, N.B.," or indeed your late brother's Bankers (69 Pall Mall) have always an acct. with me too—but, before going to the actual finis in this matter, there is something I will crave to mention, which has risen to my mind on occasion of it, and to which I must beg your serious attention for my sake.

I knew generally, or understood, long since by some casual hint or transient question to me by him whom we have lost, that the bulk of his property (after an event which it was not likely I should ever witness) was to go in

literary charities.   I think he said to
the Literary Fund.   And once again,
long afterwards, I remember to have
heard him speak, in reply to some
question of mine, about your brother
William's commercial misfortunes.   Now
if it be that there is any lack, or change
of such in that latter quarter, permit me
to urge with emphasis that, as there is
no shadow of it here, it would gratify
me in a much higher and richer degree
if I might be permitted to lay down
there the actual sum of money in
question; retaining ever the soul and
essence of it; which would be among
the perennial jewels of my life, more
precious far than any gold!

Forgive me for urging this on your
most candid, impartial and deliberate
consideration.   For it is a fact, quietly
certain as any on the banker's ledger,
that this, (if the above surmise have
any basis at all) is the mode of disposal
which would enrich me most.   And I
will say no more of it here, but
solemnly leave it with you.

Or if you wished to exchange a few

words on it with me, as you daily go driving for health, you can nearly every day find me here, till 3 p.m. and after 8 p.m. I leave it with you, but I consider it a thing that greatly and even sacredly concerns us both.—Yours always with many sympathies and thanks,

T. CARLYLE.

H. F. Chorley, Esq.

OF RECLAIMING LAND—IRISH LABOURERS.

Of reclaiming land and bogs in the Highlands, Carlyle said to me that, as far as he could learn, it took about £12 per acre to clear out the stones and make it begin to be serviceable. That to bring in land was a true and lasting good; but it needed real work. Not the kind of performance he had once seen in Ireland, where a gang of la-

E

bourers stood, each of them leisurely turning up two ounces of earth and throwing it against heaven, with a little shovel, into which was stuck a long pole, instead of an ordinary spade-handle; and all these men, said he, were well paid for doing nothing.

OF FOWLS AND EGGS.

Economics led him to speak of rearing fowls and engaging in egg culture, which he maintained was too much neglected in this country, and might be made a very profitable business investment.

OF RIVERS.

Leaving that subject, he discoursed of rivers roaring down amid granite rocks, in thundering volume, and white

with seething foam; parenthetically interpolating, in a lower tone of voice—
" Like Irish rebellion ! "

He said he liked rivers ; but when he makes inquiries about those he passes, when travelling, people look, if they do not say, " What does the old curmudgeon mean ? " For they only want the railway station.

Having given us his opinion of parliamentary eloquence and the Reform Bill, in a few terse, caustic phrases, and reminded us of his queries regarding land culture, we bade him adieu. Leaving Chelsea at a quarter to eleven o'clock, we strolled cityward by the riverside for half an hour, beneath the stars, recalling what we had that evening heard, before we could think of hailing and entering a cab.

ANOTHER VISIT WITH DR. ANGUS SMITH—CARLYLE'S SAD LOOK.

In February, 1869, Dr. Angus Smith, who came up to town on purpose that we might make some visits together, again accompanied me to Chelsea. We there found Miss Mary Carlyle Aitken, who kept house for her uncle, and Miss Welsh, a relative of the late Mrs. Carlyle, who was on a visit from Scotland.

When Miss Aitken used to visit us in Scotland, my boys naturally abridged her name (Mary Aitken) into " Maiken," and so we never called her anything else. Carlyle was asleep when we called ; but, remembering his weary looks on a former occasion, I would not allow his niece to disturb him. Soon, however, he came in of his own accord, for he expected us.

His countenance wore at times, especially since his wife's death, the quiet,
subdued, melancholy look of a man who
had not long to live, and knew it—looking the while wistfully forward to his
release.

HIS MOODS DEPENDENT ON HIS OBTAINING SLEEP.

The mood would change; and there
appeared an infinite depth of tenderness
and sweet humanity in him, blended
with prodigious power, and dashed with
irrepressible sallies of a quiet, grim,
almost weird humour, *sui generis.*

If he had fortunately succeeded in
obtaining a fair quantum of sleep
during the previous night, friends
calling would find him gentle, kind,
and communicative, taking an interest

in everything human that came across him.

GOVERNMENT MISMANAGERS.

This evening he was indignant at those he called "the Government *mis-managers*—Bright, Gladstone & Co."; talked of the bottle-nosed whale hoax; and of Fenians.

In reference to wordy, wind-bag, misleading, parliamentary oratory, he said: —"What does it matter how well a man speaks, provided that which he says is not true?"

ILLUSTRATES THE ROMAN CATHOLIC QUESTION BY A STORY.

The Roman Catholic question, he thus quaintly illustrated, after Lincoln's fashion, by a story:

" I come into my room," said he,
" and find it overrun with rats. They
are swarming over the floor, the chairs,
sofas—rats hungry and ravenous ; rats
here, there, and everywhere! Wishing
to live at peace and be on good
friendly, or, at least, neighbourly terms,
I make a proposition to them in this
style : ' Rats,' say I, ' here is my cheese
and here is my bacon. I wish to do
fairly by you. Suppose we come to an
understanding. I shall cut the cheese
and the bacon, each right down the
middle. The one half shall be yours
and the other half mine.' No objection
is offered and the paction is made and
*r*atified. (Carlyle very seldom conde-
scended to a pun.) The rats speedily
devour their own share ; but, when that
is done, they immediately proceed to
eat up mine, and, if this kind of thing

be allowed to go on, they certainly will
not stop till they have not only finished
all the cheese and bacon, but have
picked our skeletons clean into the
bargain. *That* is what the rats are
bent on doing. It is not a share they
want, but all; and the disestablishment
of the Irish Church is a breaking down
of barriers, a making way for the rats;
and, consequently, tends to sweep away
religion itself, where a little more of
that preserving salt is greatly needed at
the present time.

DYSPEPSIA SINCE 1818.

He reverted to Dixon, the Sunderland corkcutter, and to certain information we had procured for him; after
which he made some touching allusions
to his own early days—his student life,

his mental struggle and anxieties about
entering the Church, and about
temporalities, and his constant tor-
ture, more or less, from dyspepsia,
ever since 1818 ; but there was, he
said, organically or otherwise, nothing
else wrong with him.

LONDON LITERARY LIFE.

He spoke strongly of the undesirable-
ness of a London literary life—its worries,
plagues, and botherations; its utter hurt-
fulness to peace of mind and body ; and
its general uselessness, as things go. He
had known and quaintly described to us
Buckingham, Dilke, and several others.

SANITARY MATTERS.

Health led him to touch on sanitary
matters, and he alluded to the pollution

of rivers which converted them into fluid abominations of mud and sluggish black horror.

LONELY SADNESS.

There was a tone of unutterable and lonely sadness in the way he spoke of himself as a poor, worn out, well nigh done individual, who had not long to be here, but who looked forward to a better world of realities; for this world, said he, now and for long, to him had been very full of suffering of all kinds.

TRUTH AND RELIGION.

He spoke with great reverence of truth and religion, without which, he said, society would become disintegrated and speedily fall into dust.

FREDERICK'S SHORTCOMINGS AND GOOD QUALITIES.

He regretted that Frederick, unlike Cromwell, had no religion at all, and less theology. He (Frederick) owed what measure of success he had, simply to his sticking to facts, as he could apprehend them; and to his, so far, unconsciously falling in with God's ways, when working out his own ideas of right. He (Frederick) wanted to have realities.

SHAMS—WOODEN NUTMEGS—FALSE LIFE-BUOYS.

Carlyle said—shams were shamefully common, not confined to any particular walk, and instanced life-buoys stuffed with shavings, instead of cork. Wooden nutmegs, he added, were bad enough; but in that case the badness was only negative, while the Mammon-loving cheats, who palmed off the worst kind of such damnable falsities for life-buoys, were the worst kind of treacherous murderers, and hanging was too good for them.

A PLAN FOR WALKING ON THE WATER.

He then described a plan for walking on water of which he was cognizant. It was devised long ago, by a working man, who, just because ignorant, was very confident of success. Accordingly, he invited his comrades to witness a performance which was to demonstrate man's power over the elements and the non-necessity, in future, of such a thing as death by drowning.

The hour arrived. Some sort of clumsy cork apparatus was fastened to

each foot, and when everything had
been adjusted entirely to his own satisfaction, he said: "Now see! Here is
the thing! Look!" And, like Peter,
he stepped boldly on to the water; but,
unlike Peter, with arms extended, he at
once wheeled over, head down and
corked feet up, in accordance with the
general laws of gravity, which did not
choose in this particular case to make
an exception in his favour. Thus, in-
verted and irretrievably perpendicular,
he would have remained, without other
help than his own. That, however, soon
reached him, and he was ignominiously
fished out, a wetter if not a wiser man.

CARLYLE SMOKING.

Carlyle, in his gray dressing-gown,
sat part of that evening on the floor, on

the hearth-rug by the fireside, smoking
a new long clay pipe, and kept puffing
the smoke up the chimney.   He said he
smoked in great moderation, and did
not allow himself to exceed by a single
"*draw*" what he knew by experience
would be helpful to him.   Everything
that affected his stomach had to be
carefully attended to, under pains and
penalties, which in his case were inex-
orably exacted, if he transgressed by a
hair's breadth.

CARLYLE ON HIS OWN PROFILE.

Sitting there, he spoke of the profile
portrait of himself, which is engraved as
a frontispiece in some recent editions of
his works, that for which Woolner, the
sculptor, when on a visit to Scotland in
1868, told me he had posed Carlyle,

when the photograph was being taken, in order that he might get the ear done for modelling purposes. " Judges consider it," said Carlyle, " the perfection of a likeness of me ; but I, who for some forty years, more or less, daily performed a certain barbarous operation, although that same is given up now, and looked in a mirror on these occasions, would not know that I had ever before looked upon that man."

As two mirrors are requisite for seeing one's own profile, few people know what it is like.

WOOLNER'S BUST AND MEDALLION OF HIM.

Woolner executed a bust of Carlyle, an excellent likeness, which, in order to be seen to the best advantage, the sculptor told me, should be placed a little higher than the line, so that the eye of a person looking at it may be on a level with the mouth of the bust. Woolner also executed a fine medallion of Carlyle.

ON A PHOTOGRAPH OF HIMSELF.

Of another photograph, Carlyle remarked—that he was certainly shaggy enough, in all conscience, without being made worse than he really was; but that this likeness made him look like an old rascally, ruffian, obfuscated goose!

THE BLACK COUNTRY.

The Welsh iron mines and the Black Country generally he epigrammatically described as "Chaos plus gold"; but added, that the furnaces helped him to realize scenes in Dante's "Inferno."

LIBRARY EDITION—WALK TO THE CITY.

He showed us a new volume of the library edition of his works which is being issued. It was a glorious moonlight night, when Dr. Angus Smith and I left to walk to our hotel, in order that we might, by the way, recall the panoramic and wonderful discourse to which we had been delightedly listening.

WALK IN THE PARK—CHELSEA—GERMAN CARE OF TREES—THE NORTH.

On Friday evening, August 13, 1869, I visited Chelsea alone. Found " Maiken." After partaking of some refreshment, Carlyle asked me to take a walk with him, and we strolled up to the

F

Park.   He talked of the former country
aspect of Chelsea, when he first came to
it; but now it is so built in.   He spoke
of the impolicy of cutting down trees
that take five hundred years to grow, as
utilitarian folly and the work of Goths.
He commended the German Government for educating woodmen and enact-
ing that trees should be planted to re-
place those cut down.

Then he talked of Iceland, and of the
old Scandinavian mythology, of Thor,
and Odin.

OF HIS HOUSE—OF GOOD AND SCAMPED BUILDINGS.

Referring to his house, built in the
reign of Queen Anne, he discoursed of
good and bad bricks, remarking that
analogous disintegrating processes went

on in society. His words so closely re-
sembled one of his published utterances
regarding "cheap and nasty" that I
substitute it here, rather than follow my
own memoranda :

"London bricks are reduced to dry
clay again in the course of sixty years
or sooner. *Bricks*, burn them rightly,
build them faithfully, with mortar faithfully tempered, they will stand, I believe, barring earthquakes and cannon,
for 6000 years, if you like! Etruscan
pottery (*baked clay*, but rightly baked)
is some 3000 years of age and still fresh
as an infant. Truly, the state of London
house-building, at this time—who shall
express how detestible it is, how fright-
ful! England needs to be *rebuilt* once
every seventy years. Build it once
rightly, the expense will be, say, fifty per
cent. more; but every seventy years we

shall save the cost of building all England over again ? "

He then said people long ago built houses intending that their great-grandchildren should inhabit them, instead of running up whole streets of scamped brick-and-a-half shells, with no allowance for dancing, which to a certainty would detach the joists and bring down the floors, with the whole concern tumbling about their ears.

ECCLEFECHAN STORY TO ILLUSTRATE THE OLD SCOTCH PREFERENCE FOR FREEHOLD INSTEAD OF LEASE.

A seventy-seven or ninety-nine-years lease seemed to satisfy people in London; but in Scotland, in his young days, folks liked to build on freehold ground, unrestrictedly their own.

In illustration of this laudable trait,

he narrated an amusing story of an
old tailor who used to come to his
parents' house, situated in Matthew
Murray's Close, at Ecclefechan, in
order to "make down" his father's
clothes into *quasi* new suits for his
brothers and himself. The wages paid
to the tailor were a shilling a day and
his victuals. He well remembered his
arriving in the morning, and fetching
with him a round sod of turf, about as
large as the top of a little table. This
he placed on the floor, stuck a stick into
it, with a slit split on the top, which
held a candle like a vice, and there the
tailor sat on the floor, from morning to
night, barring meal times, and worked
away.

This man, by dint of great industry
and saving, had amassed a little money,
and his special ambition was to be-

come a laird, by purchasing the house in which he lived; but it so happened that the owner of the house, who had also made his money in the same slow, sure way, wanted to drive a hard bargain and obtain a good price for it. So negotiations went on for four years, more or less, between the two high contracting parties, as if it had been a treaty between two of the great European Powers.

At length, the matter so far took shape that a meeting was held, at which each was represented by a lawyer, and a draft deed was produced. On its being begun to be read aloud, "I, John So-and-So [both the names escaped my memory], hereby agree to let, lease, etc., for 999 years," the tailor at once struck in with, " What is that you say about letting and leasing? I tell you what it is, I'll hae naething adae wi' the transaction ava, unless I can buy the house *out and out to a' eternity!* "

The one lawyer, seeing they had got a character to deal with, gave a knowing look to the other, who represented the tailor, and, anxious to expedite business, said, " Well, now, suppose we add a 9 figure to it, and then see how it reads : "I, John ——, hereby let, lease, etc., for 9999 years.' " And, with great difficulty, after much persuasion, said Carlyle, they at length got him to entertain and accept of these amended terms!

POOR ORGAN-GRINDERS.

Hearing a street organ, he remarked that, although the noise of that and

such like disturbed and irritated him
when at work, he had much sympathy
with the poor lads who ground them.
They were mostly a harmless, ill-used
set, strangers here in a foreign land,
bound to cruel masters, who gave them
porridge in the morning and a flogging
at night, if they did'nt fetch back as
much cash as satisfied the inhuman
monster who lent the organ and sent
them out.

RUSKIN'S "QUEEN OF THE AIR"—THE HOUSE FLY—RUSKIN'S UPBRINGING.

That evening, on going in, I had
found Carlyle reading Ruskin's " Queen
of the Air." He strongly recommended
me to get it, adding, that—leaving out
his mode of accounting for the mytho-
logical parts relating to Pomona,

Minerva, etc., and coming to actualities
and the present state of things—it was
all deeply and tragically true. He said
it contained some of the very best and
truest things. The passage on liberty
and the house-fly Carlyle read aloud to
me, marching about the room and de-
claiming it with great gusto, declaring
that he thought it true to the very core,
an illustration happy all through, and
altogether one of the most wonderful
bits of dramatic, natural, and powerful
prose writing in the English language.
Here it is :—

" I believe we can nowhere find a
better type of a perfectly free creature
than in the common house-fly. Not
free only, but brave; and irreverent to
a degree which I think no human
republican could by any philosophy
exalt himself to. There is no courtesy
in him; he does not care whether it is

king or clown whom he teases; and in
every step of his swift mechanical
march, and in every pause of his
resolute observation, there is one and
the same expression of perfect egotism,
perfect independence and self-confi-
dence, and conviction of the world's
having been made for flies. Strike at
him with your hand, and to him the
mechanical fact and external aspect of
the matter is, what to you it would be,
if an acre of red clay, ten feet thick,
tore itself up from the ground in one
massive field, hovered over you in the
air for a second, and then came crash-
ing down with an aim. That is the
external aspect of it; the inner aspect,
to his fly's mind, is of a quite natural
and unimportant occurrence—one of
the momentary conditions of his active
life. He steps out of the way of your
hand, and alights on the back of it.
You cannot terrify him, nor govern him,
nor persuade him, nor convince him.
He has his own positive opinion on all
matters—not an unwise one, usually,
for his own ends—and will ask no

advice of yours. He has no work to do, no tyrannical instinct to obey. The earthworm has his digging; the bee, her gathering and building; the spider, her cunning net-work; the ant, her treasury, and accounts. All these are comparatively slaves, or people of vulgar business. But your fly, free in the air, free in the chamber—a black incarnation of caprice—wandering, investigating, flitting, flirting, feasting at his will, with rich variety of choice in feast, from the heaped sweets in the grocer's window to those of the butcher's back-yard, and from the galled place on your cab-horse's back, to the brown spot on the road, from which, as the hoof disturbs him, he rises with angry republican buzz — what freedom is like his?"*

Carlyle added, that when Ruskin stuck to facts, and looked at things as they

---

* "Queen of The Air," p.p. 170-2. Paragraph No. 148.

were known to men, or described scenes
in Nature, he was great and had prodigious power. He had seen and admired
some of his designs for houses, and he
sketched and planned well. He (Ruskin),
said the Sage, owed much to his famil-
iarity with the Bible, and to his having
been carefully brought up by pious
Presbyterian parents on both sides of
of the house.

*HOW HE GOT HIS BROTHER DR. JOHN
    A. CARLYLE TO BEGIN HIS TRANS-
    LATION OF DANTE.*

While walking in Rotten Row, he told
me how his brother John, who had been
twenty years in Italy, as physician to
the Duke of Buccleuch, had amassed
an enormous amount of Dante material
toward executing a prose translation,

For long he had unsuccessfully urged
his brother to set about it ; but, urge
and progue as he would, he could not
get him to begin.   So he resolved on
trying quite another plan, and bethought
him of the man who was driving pigs to
Killarney, and who told his friend to
hush and speak low, for the pigs thought
he wanted them to go the other wáy.
This story he told with great animation,
standing still the while and acting it
inimitably, saying, after he had finished :
" *That* was how I got John to begin his
translation, and thus it came about.   One
day, said I : 'John, man, if I were in your
shoes, I would get quit of that Dante
business, which hangs about your neck
like a dead albatross.   Cast it away from
you and give up all thought of ever
translating Dante.   If you had been a
young man, you might have looked for-

ward to overtaking it; but now you are *too old*. Read, and enjoy yourself, and bother your head no more about Dante.'"

" The steel struck fire," said Carlyle, " as was intended. John exclaimed : ' ME *too old !* I'm nothing of the kind !' And so, forthwith, he set to work, and produced one of the very best translations of Dante to be found anywhere."

OF EDWARD IRVING.

Speaking of his early friend, Edward Irving, for whom he had the greatest admiration and love—saying that as a friendly man and brother he never expected to look on his like again—he mentioned that the origin of his squint was the fact of there being a little window on one side of his cradle. As he grew up, Irving saw two things and made an effort to see only one, but could not quite over-come it all his life. If a candle were burning before him, he saw it, and another dim one beside it.

He asked me to find out for him what medical man attended Irving in Glasgow, and to obtain for him some particulars about his last illness and death. These I obtained from the late Dr. Rainey, forwarded to Chelsea, and received from Carlyle a letter of thanks expressing his entire satisfaction with the way in which all his wishes had therewith been met.

HOW HE CHOSE TO WRITE ABOUT FREDERICK.

In referring to " Frederick," he said, that he was necessitated to go over so many tons of sheer rubbish that he often felt as if he were searching for a needle in a hay-stack; yet he could not tell what these tons might possibly contain till he had examined them all.   As for his making choice of this subject, he said that he had long felt that the tide of democracy was fast hurrying us along downward; so he cast his eyes about seeking for a man that could rule, in order that he might hold him up, in that respect, as an example, and so do what he could to stem the current. Frederick, at that time, seemed to him the last of the Romans, and so he took him for his text.   As the study went on, he found reason to modify his opinion of Frederick somewhat, and perhaps it would have been better to have taken up Luther or Knox, on other grounds; but, having put his hand to the plough, he dared not look back, but proceeded to set down the very truth about him and his times, good or bad, as far as he possibly could ascertain it.

OF HIS ILLEGIBLE, CRAMPED, AND INTRICATELY INTERPOLATED MANUSCRIPT.

Portions of the MS. of "Frederick," which I saw and examined, were written by an amanuensis, but were largely interpolated with Carlyle's own writing. I can sympathize with the printers who had to set it, and who, on account of the numerous corrections and alterations which he made on his proofs, sometimes found it easier to reset the whole than correct them as they stood. Dr. Carlyle told me a story of a compositor in this connection; but, as it is also related by Miss Martineau, I shall quote

G

from her fuller version, substantially the same as the Doctor's, with this difference, in the denoument, that the latter represented the man as at once putting on his hat and bolting from the office :

"One day," said Miss Martineau, " while in my study, I heard a prodigious sound of laughter on the stairs, and in came Carlyle, laughing aloud. He had been laughing in that manner all the way from the printing office in Charing Cross. As soon as he could, he told me what it was about. He had been to the office to urge on the printer, and the man said : ' Why, sir, you really are so very hard upon us with your corrections. They take so much time, you see.' After some remonstrance, Carlyle observed that he had been accustomed to this sort of thing; that he had got works printed in Scotland and ——.

'Yes, indeed, sir, interrupted the printer; we are aware of that. We have a man here from Edinburgh, and when he took up a bit of your copy he dropped it as if it had burnt his fingers, and cried out: Lord have mercy! Have you got that man to print for? Lord knows when we shall get done all his corrections!'"

HIS DRESS.

Carlyle that evening was dressed in a black shooting-coat and vest, gray trousers, and wore a soft felt whitish-gray wide-awake hat, with a band of crape on it. He had, for neck-gear, a stiff, high, black, old-fashioned stock, with a buckle fastening it behind; a turned-down collar; and his beard white, grizzly, and protruding.

At the Marble Arch, as we walked, a

number of people stopped and looked at him, evidently recognising the Sage by his portraits.

MOVEMENTS — CORDIAL INVITATION.

He said he much wished to sail somewhere with his brother for a few weeks. To-morrow, he goes to say "Good-bye" to Lady Ashburton; and his brother the Doctor is to arrive on Monday.

He is curious to see an old Icelandic Saga which I have in MS., and hopes to visit me, if at all in my neighbourhood.

He kindly asked me to come again next day; and, if I could make up my mind to rest with him over Sunday, his niece would stay at home that day.

He was particularly kind, gentle, and friendly, insisting on my staying later; but I had duties during the day and needed rest, so, bidding him adieu, "Maiken" accompanied me to a Thames steamer, and saw me off for Paul's Wharf.

That was my last visit to Great Cheyne Row, and I saw Carlyle no more.

CONCLUSION.

Such are some stray jottings, with records of a few out of many visits to Chelsea. In them, Carlyle's remarks, as well as my own personal impressions of him, are faithfully although disjointedly reproduced. Differing *in toto* from his views in regard to slavery, and his mistaken estimates of some men; of his deep reverence and entire sincerity there can be no question.

For example, Carlyle and Wordsworth —although two of the greatest thinkers of the age—not only did not understand each other's characteristic greatness, but were intellectually quite repellant to each other.

When, in Wordsworth's latter days, Carlyle met him in London, he fully recognised his strong intellect, his veracity, dignity, shrewd insight, and marvellous power in presenting striking delineations of character. But, beyond such recognition, Carlyle was quite at sea in regard to Wordsworth's position as a poet; for, loving action, Carlyle cared little for meditative poetry, or indeed for modern poetry of any kind— always excepting Burns—so that the *form*, in this case, repelled him from even considering the *substance*.

When he could not see, he rashly

concluded that there was nothing to be seen; and so, at times, he was grievously mistaken ; as in his views on what he called " the Nigger question." However, to do him justice here, it was not to colour or race he objected, so much as to certain traits which he associated with these; wrongly believing them to be inherent and incurable, instead of being naturally induced by an infamous system of outrageous wrong, which has been truly called " the sum of all villanies"; traits, for which, wherever found, he would have prescribed the same drastic remedies, for white or black.

So too, in his under-estimates of men like Coleridge, Charles Lamb, and others; although, on the other hand, where one would have least expected it, he could appreciate Leigh Hunt, and Mazzini.

Work is good, but *Thought* precedes it, is higher, guides and controls it.

Wordsworth, again, who attached great importance to artistic form, as well as to the subject matter in hand, revering the "wells of English undefiled," was, in turn, decidedly repelled by the unwonted, often uncouth, through-at-the-nearest, but very forcible modes of expression employed by the Sage of Chelsea, whose main requirement of the *how* was—that it should hit the *what*.

Thus it came about, that, from taking different stand-points, these two men— master-spirits who have so largely influenced and, shaped the thought-currents of the age—curiously enough, repelled each other, while we, who look back, are truly thankful for them both.

In conclusion, allow me to append two characteristic passages: the first from Carlyle's published works, setting forth the very practical nature of his philosophy; and the second from a letter, also already in print, to his friend Erskine of Linlathen, and finely illustrating his unfeigned faith, humble spirit, and Christian character.

" THE STRONG MAN.

" Of conquest we may say that it never yet went by brute force and compulsion; conquest of that kind does not endure. Conquest, along with power of compulsion, an essential universally in human society, must bring benefit along with it, or men of the ordinary strength of men will fling it out. The strong man, what is he if we will consider? The wise man;

the man with the gift of method, of faith-
fulness and valour, all of which are the
basis of wisdom ; who has insight into
what is what, into what will follow out
of what, the eye to see and the hand to
do; who is *fit* to administer, to direct, and
guidingly command : he is the strong
man.   His muscles and bones are no
stronger than ours ; but his soul is
stronger, his soul is wiser, clearer,—is
better and nobler, for that is, has been,
and ever will be the root of all clearness
worthy of such a name.   Beautiful it is,
and a gleam from the same eternal pole-
star visible amid the destinies of men,
that all talent, all intellect is in the first
place moral;—what a world it would be
otherwise !   But it is the heart always
that sees, before the head *can* see : let
us know that ; and know therefore that
the good alone is deathless and victor-
ious ; that Hope is sure and steadfast, in
all phases of this 'Place of Hope. Shifti-
ness, quirk, attorney-cunning is a thing
that fancies itself, and is often fancied to
be talent ; but it is luckily mistaken in
that.   Succeed truly it does, what is

called succeeding; and even must in general succeed it the dispensers of success be of due stupidity: men of due stupidity will needs say to it '*Thou* art wisdom; rule Thou!' Whereupon it rules.

"But Nature answers: 'No, this ruling of thine is not according to *my* laws; thy wisdom was not wise enough! Dost thou take me too for a Quackery, for a Conventionality and Attorneyism? This chaff that thou sowest into my bosom, though it pass at the poll-booth and elsewhere for seed-corn, *I* will not grow wheat out of it, for it is chaff!" *

LETTER TO MR. ERSKINE OF LINLATHEN.

"CHELSEA, February 12th, 1869.
"DEAR MR. ERSKINE:—I was most agreeably surprised by the sight of your

---

* "Chartism," Chapter V. [Library Edition, Vol. X., p. 359].

handwriting again, so kind, so welcome.
The letters are as firm and honestly
distinct as ever. The mind, too, in spite
of its frail *environments*, as clear, *plumb-
up*, calmly expectant as in the best days.
Right so. So be it with us all, till we
quit this dim sojourn, now grown so
lonely to us, and our change come!
' Our Father, which art in Heaven,
hallowed be thy name, thy will be done '
—what else can we say? The other
night, in my sleepless tossings about,
which were growing more and more
miserable, these words, that brief and
grand prayer, came strangely into my
mind, with an altogether new emphasis,
as if *written*, and shining for me in mild,
pure splendour on the black bosom of
the night there, when I, as it were, *read.*
them word by word, with a sudden check
to my imperfect wanderings, with a
sudden softness of composure, which was
much unexpected. Not for perhaps
thirty or forty years had I once formally
repeated that prayer. Nay, I never felt
before how intensely the voice of man's
soul it is; the inmost aspiration of all

that is high and pious in poor human
nature, right worthy to be recommended
with an 'After this manner pray ye.' .
. . All my little work is henceforth
private (as I calculate)—a setting of my
poor house in order, which I fain would
finish *in time*, and occasionally fear I
shan't. Dear Mr. Erskine, good be ever
with you. Were my hand *as little shaky*
as it is to-day, I would write to you
oftener. A word *from* you will ever be
welcome here.

"Yours, sincerely and much,

"T. CARLYLE."